THIS CANDLEWICK BOOK BELONGS TO:

_____

_____

_____

For Leroy

and his story

Also with love and thanks to my friends—

Tricia, Melanie,

Frank (especially for coediting late at night in Cork),

Carolyn, Kate, Helen,

Paul and Sybille,

and to Mark and Bonzo across the alleyway

Also to Cathryn

This story is based in and around
Salisbury Road and Beaumont Park,
Plymouth, England. Ordinary life.
Warmest thanks to Michael Hill
and to Helen Read at Walker Books.

Copyright © 1997 by Simon James

First U.S. paperback edition in this format 2016

The Library of Congress has cataloged the hardcover edition as follows:

James, Simon.
Leon and Bob / Simon James. — 1st U.S. ed.
Summary: Leon and his imaginary friend, Bob, do everything together until a new boy moves in next door.
ISBN 978-1-56402-991-1 (hardcover)
[1. Imaginary playmates — Fiction. 2. Friendship — Fiction.
3. Blacks — England — Fiction. 4. England — Fiction.] I. Title.
PZ7.J1544Le   1997
[E] — dc20   96-2684

ISBN 978-0-7636-2686-0 (original paperback)
ISBN 978-0-7636-8175-3 (reformatted paperback)

APS 21 20 19 18
10 9 8 7 6 5 4 3

Printed in Humen, Dongguan, China

This book was typeset in Goudy.
The illustrations were done in watercolor and ink.

Candlewick Press
99 Dover Street
Somerville, Massachusetts 02144

visit us at www.candlewick.com

Leon and Bob

Simon James

CANDLEWICK PRESS

Leon had moved into town
with his mom.
His dad was away in the army.
Leon shared his room
with his new friend, Bob.

No one else could see Bob,
but Leon knew he was there.
Leon always laid a place
for Bob at the table.
"More milk, Bob?" Leon said.

Sometimes Leon's mom
couldn't take Leon to school,
but Leon didn't mind.
He always walked to school with Bob.
He always had Bob to talk to.

Often, when Leon got home,
there was a letter waiting for him
from his dad.
Bob liked to hear Leon read it
over and over again.

One Saturday, Leon heard
some noises in the street below.
He saw a new family moving in
next door.
A boy looked up at Leon and waved.
Leon waved back.

The next day Leon and Bob
ate their breakfast
very quickly.
Then Leon grabbed his ball
and rushed outside.

Leon ran up the steps
of the house next door.
He was about halfway
when suddenly he realized
Bob wasn't there anymore.

Leon sat down.

He was all alone.

He could ring the bell

or he could go home.

Why wasn't Bob there

to help him?

Leon rang the bell
and waited.
The door opened.
"Hello," said the boy.
"H-hello," said Leon.
"Would you like to go to the park?"

"Okay," said the boy.

"I'm just going to the park, Mom,"
he called.

Together Leon and the boy walked
down the steps toward the street.

"My name's Leon," said Leon.

"What's yours?"

"Bob," said Bob.

Simon James began drawing at an early age, taking inspiration from his father's collection of books on cartoonists like Ronald Searle and Gerard Hoffnung. Though he wanted to become a cartoonist, his university education in graphic design and art history led him down the path to becoming a children's book illustrator and the publication of his first book, *The Day Jake Vacuumed*, in 1989. His many other books for children include the best-selling *Dear Mr. Blueberry; Baby Brains; Little One Step; Nurse Clementine;* and *Days Like This: A Collection of Small Poems*, which was short-listed for the Kate Greenaway Medal. Simon James's books have been published in more than twenty languages around the world. He lives in England, where he continues to write and illustrate full-time.